Clarion Books
a Houghton Mifflin Company imprint
215 Park Avenue South, New York, NY 10003
Copyright © 2004 by Albin Michel Jeunesse
Originally published in France in 2004 under the title *Je m'ennuie*.
First American edition, 2006

The illustrations were executed in pastel.
The text was set in 18-point Eureka.

www.houghtonmifflinbooks.com

Printed in Singapore

Library of Congress Cataloging-in-Publication Data

ISBN-13: 978-0-618-65760-5
ISBN-10: 0-618-65760-6
LC#: 2005021167
Full Cataloging information is available from the Library of Congress.

10 9 8 7 6 5 4 3

Christine Schneider
Hervé Pinel

I'm Bored!

Clarion Books
New York

"Mom, I'm bored."
"Go play with Katherine, Charlie."
"She won't let me. She says I'm too little."

7

"Dad, I'm bored."

"Go have fun, and don't bother me!"

Sunday afternoon
is like a rainy day.
Boring!
When I can't watch TV
or use the computer,
I'm bored.
I hate being bored,
but sometimes I can't help it.

"Ow!"
"Oops, sorry . . .

. . . Teddy! You can talk?"
"Yes, I can talk. But you don't listen anymore!
All you do is sulk. I get nothing—not a hug, not
even a tickle! I'm bored!"

"*Hey!*"

"Robot! You can talk too?"

"Yes, I can talk, but do you listen? Not anymore. You just complain all the time. I get nothing, not even a 'Buzz buzz!' I'm bored!"

"*Hee-haw!*"
"You can talk too, Donkey?"
"Yes, I can talk, but the only thing you listen to anymore is your own grumbling. I get nothing, not even a 'Giddyup!' I'm bored!"

"Charlie, what are you doing?"

"I'm going to get rid of Boredom!
Follow me, men! Let's plan our attack!"

"We'll start with the desk. It's bored to death."

"I've got some books, Charlie!"
"And I've got some socks."
"And here are the balls."
"Good work, everyone!"

"Desk, you be the Monster Who Eats Boredom. Okay, Teddy?"
"He's really scary."
"Robot, Donkey . . . report in."

"We're saving your soldiers . . . from Boredom."
"Everyone, up that hill! Castle, you guard the high ground!"

"Castle is the fortress that protects us from Boredom!
How's that sound, troops?"

"Great!"

"Terrific!"

"Teddy, report in."

"I've been to the kitchen."
"What for?"

"To get helmets and shields."
"Well done, Teddy!"

"Surround the closet!
Boredom is hiding in there.
To your stations!"
"Yes, Charlie!"
"Helmets on?"
"Yes, Charlie!"
"Weapons ready?"
"Yes, Charlie!"
"Desk and Castle, you're on the
alert?"
"Yes, Charlie!"
"Shh! I hear Boredom coming!"

"Ready . . ."

"Charge!"

"Charlie, what's going on in here?"

"Um . . ."
"Charlie?"
"I'm just playing."

"Charlie, you've made a mess of this whole room!"

"No, I haven't. That part over there is clean. Besides, clean stuff is boring. But I know how to keep boredom away. If we play something, we won't get bored!"

"Mom, it's your turn. Are you daydreaming?"
"No, I'm just looking at all of the . . . not boring part."
"Don't worry, Mom. I'll clean it up—
next Sunday afternoon."